Threads of THE WAR

Threads
of

THE WAR

Volume IV

Personal Truth-Inspired Flash-Fiction
of *the 20th Century's War*

A Collection of Historical Short Stories by:

JEREMYSTROZER

Threads of The War, Volume IV

By Jeremy Strozer

Published by The Good Enough Empire, LLC.

Falls Church, VA 22043 USA

All photograph source links were current at the time of publication.

Jeremy Strozer

ISBN: 978-099-943010-1

Contents

Acknowledgements

None of these stories would have been written without the encouragement of my wife, Jan, whose support and energy drives me to share my passion with the world.

I would not have restarted my passion for writing if not for my son, Joshua, whose innocence and earnestness compels me to want to eliminate the idea of war from the human condition. Every story I tell is an attempt to, in my own way, change the world and potentially save my son from suffering through such catastrophe, let alone participate in one. I also want to demonstrate to Joshua how people can do what they most love in life, even if they must hold down a full-time job while they are doing it. I want him to know he can follow his passions no matter what else in life is going on.

My mother-in-law, Linda Stennett, continues to provide inspiration and nurturing support as I transition to become a focused author. Her help all these years is what enabled me even to start sharing my writing in the first place.

Through their encouragement and support, the following people helped form this book: Donald (Pat) Patierno, Shulamit Widawsky, Joshua Spero, Sean Kay, David Seminera, Adam Meyer, Paula Killen, Scott Whitehair, and Nadine Warner.

How this book looks and feels is attributable to the dedicated hard work of my editor, Deb Ling. She turned a collection of missives in MS Word into a final product available to the world.

Finally, I would like to thank my BETA readers Denis Yaro, Emilio Iasiello, Richard Saunders, and Caitlin Rourk. Their comments, suggestions, edits, and ideas made this book far better than the one I presented to them originally. Without their help, I could not turn these stories from simple ideas into compelling prose for others to desire reading.

Introduction

Pulled from the tapestry of history, what follows this introduction are threads of The 20th Century's War. These small strands of life experience open our eyes to the personal and emotional drama of modern warfare. Each thread offers insight into how individuals encounter, and sometimes overcome, industrial and post-industrial state-sponsored violence.

In this fourth volume of selected stories from The 20th Century's War, you will encounter remorse, retribution, shame, surprise, confusion, hatred, bravery, honor, dishonor, and more. As you read these stories, please think of all who were involved in The 20th Century's War and how you interact with each of them every day. This war lives in all of us. Let us never forget how we got here. Let us learn from this path to guide where we will go next. May the lessons of history compel the world toward Peace!

Youth

You will have me.

You will win.

I welcome you to take me.

I have won.

This mantra incessantly repeats itself in my mind. With each breath, one of four sentences, in specific order, drives forth. No more words through my mouth. No more pain. Simply a mind with four thoughts propelled forever through me.

I lay here, where I've been alone for four years, chained to the wall of Theresienstadt Prison. At one time, the chain held both of my wrists, but now it only holds one frail piece of skin and bone. Last month, my right arm was amputated because of the Tuberculosis.

I wasn't always sick. I was quite healthy my whole life until June 1914. Then, in custody, I became sick.

You will have me.

You will win.

I welcome you to take me.

I have won.

My body no longer functions, although my mind continues to haunt. I sacrificed my physical self for the freedom of my fellow countrymen. I killed a man and his wife for independence. I waste away to nothing while my dream is realized.

You will have me.

You will win.

I welcome you to take me.

I have won.

My physical form may die, but my purpose is strong. Even in youth, I will have prevailed over an ancient empire. I rise to heaven knowing my path was true.

When history reads of me, it will be of a man who freed his people from the reins of imperial rule.

You will have me.

You will win.

I welcome you to take me.

I have won.

*****

6

Gavrilo Princip died in prison on April 28, 1918 at age 23. Almost four years after he assassinated Archduke Franz Ferdinand, lighting the spark that set-off World War I, Princip was a broken man suffering from severe Tuberculosis. He'd already lost his right arm to the disease, which finally took his whole body. Had Princip been just a few months older when he committed the assassination, he would have been killed according to Austrian law. Yet, since he was under 20 years old at the time of the murder of the Archduke, Princip was sentenced to prison instead. In prison, he was kept in solitary confinement until his death. Princip's death changed nothing. The assassination he committed, which led to the deaths of many millions from war, famine, and disease set Yugoslavia free from Austrian rule, but also led to the breakup of the country he'd envisioned in the 1990s. Princip's death did not lead to a better future for his people but simply a century of war for the region. His quiet death from a broken body in a solitary cell, chained to a damp and moldy wall was based on an act that precipitated the most destructive century in human history. His death was not worth his life, or that of all the lives lost because of his action. No one won from what Princip did. No one.

Agreement

"**W**ell, that simply does not make sense," Picot flusters back at me, a little more loudly than a seasoned diplomat ought to speak.

He may be seasoned, but he's not cultured.

"It makes sense to His Majesty's Government," I retort.

This explanation should suffice for any man.

"You have negotiated with the Arabs for land that is rightly owed to the French Republic," Picot continues in the same tone.

We are in an alliance. Why are we arguing over land?

"If you wish to drag out these talks, that is your business. I wish to complete them in time for the end of the war. We can delimit our spheres of influence wherever it is most convenient for our French allies, before superimposing them upon our agreements with the Arabs."

That should quiet his restless nerves.

Smiling, he replies, "Yes, I agree with your prag-matism."

That's nice to know.

"Great, so what about this?" I offer as I lift the red grease pencil.

If a bigger piece of the Turk pie is all you want, then how about I give him a line from the "e" of Acre to the "k" of Kirkuk?

My hands press down on the well-detailed map on the wooden table before us. I stretch to reach the tip of the pencil to Acre, from which I use a ruler to draw a straight line through to Kirkuk.

How's this for pie?

"The French Republic will be most influential north of this line. His Majesty's government will be most influential south of it," I offer.

Picot, who was watching me draw the line on the map, raises his head, looking me in the eyes. His smile sits flatly on his face, as if placed there rather than formed of his own muscles.

He lifts the blue grease pencil, tracing a matching line right above the red line I just drew from Kirkuk back to Acre. Rather than stopping here, he picks up the red pencil to trace a hash mark around Palestine.

"What is that around Palestine?" I ask.

He pauses for a moment, and then announces, "An international protectorate."

Raising his head, he makes direct eye contact with me. "This will be fine."

Greedy frog! I have failed by losing Palestine.

Still eying me, he announces, "The French Republic will be happy with this settlement."

Arbitrary as it is, except for Palestine, so will His Majesty.

"Wonderful, shall we sign?" I ask, simply wanting to get this done.

How will I explain Palestine to my superiors?

"Certainly," Picot replies as he puts down the blue pencil to lift an ink-pen.

He confidently places his signature in the bottom-right corner of the map as if he expects it to be an article of long-term historical value.

I'm just happy to have these negotiations done, even if the agreement is flawed. At least I've settled the French problem.

Putting down the red pencil, I lift a wooden pencil in its place before affixing my signature just under Picot's.

This agreement won't last long enough for my signature to even matter.

*****

On May 19, 1916, representatives of the United Kingdom and France secretly reached an accord, known as the Sykes-Picot Agreement, by which most of the Arab lands under the rule of the Ottoman Empire were to be divided into British and French spheres of influence at the conclusion of World War I. Mark Sykes, an aristocrat, soldier, and member of Parliament with no experience in the region negotiated for the United Kingdom. Francois Georges-Picot, an experienced diplomat who had been stationed in Beirut and Cairo negotiated for France.

The Sykes-Picot Agreement launched a nine-year process—and other deals, declarations, and treaties—creating the modern Middle East states out of the Ottoman carcass. The new borders ultimately bore little resemblance to the original Sykes-Picot map because the British promised the same land to Arabs and Jews in multiple other agreements made around the same time to win these groups over to their side in World War I, ultimately double-crossing both groups by promising the same territory to the French.

Almost everything from the original Sykes-Picot agreement has been altered through time, duplicity, political action, and military conflict. Yet, the influence of great power rivalry in the region, which started long before World War I, cannot be disputed. To this day, great powers are still actively involved in determining the political future of the region, with the United States, Russia, and many European powers taking sides in various ongoing conflicts. While all these powers claim to be supporting stability, their intervention cannot lead to self-realized political development and security, and thus prevents regional peace.

The premise of American policy (and of every other outside power) today—in stabilizing fractious Iraq, ending Syria's gruesome civil war, and confronting the Islamic State—is to preserve the borders which evolved in the aftermath of the Sykes-Picot Agreement and the disastrous 2003 invasion of Iraq.

At some point in the future perhaps, countries will learn blowback from great power rivalry and military misadventure is far more expensive – in

terms of lives and national resources – than the initial
investment in intervention.

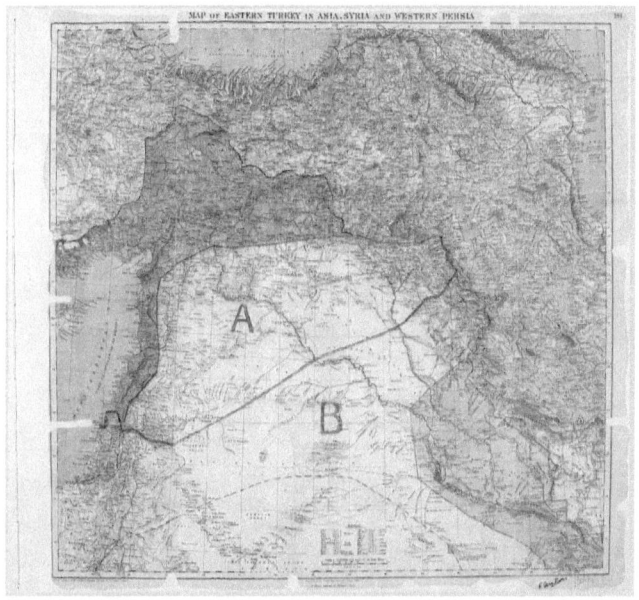

The Sykes-Picot Agreement: 1916

Sir Mark Sykes

Francois Georges Picot

Cher Ami

Taking off with precious cargo invites German fire right away.

At least let me get airborne before opening up on me, you Huns!

I bank right, hoping to avoid the barrage of small-arms fire that doomed my predecessors.

Yet, as I turn, the bullets streak past me.

My skin gets goosebumps, my eyes water, and my heart races.

How am I going to get out of here alive?

How am I going to get back to our lines?

How am I going to succeed when others failed?

I turn sharply left, attempting to zig-zag to avoid the constant fire.

Just as I finish my zag, a round clips my leg.

AAAaaarrggghhhh!

The shock of the impact sends me fluttering, as I fall to the ground.

I'm not giving up, you bastards!

Dangling from a tendon, my injured leg still

holds my precious cargo.

I'm going to make it. I'm going to get out of here! Those Huns think they shot me down.

I look up at the sky, waddle on my one good leg, and lift off again, this time aiming straight up.

I'm going to gain altitude rather than maneuver this time. I just have to get out of range fast!

The fire starts up again.

They're not giving up, neither will I!

Higher, higher, and higher still, I soar into the sky above the stranded men and those attempting to destroy them.

The Germans keep up their deadly fire as I rise above it all.

Higher, I must get higher!

A round pierces my breast bone, coming out my left eye. I lose altitude.

I don't feel the pain. I don't feel anything. I just need to get to the Command Headquarters at full speed. Nothing else matters!

The bullets stop streaking nearby.

I must be high enough!

Banking again, I head toward headquarters.

Twenty-five miles to go, just twenty-five miles.

My leg begins hurting, the bullet wound in my chest and eye stings.

I must make it, for my boys, I must make it!

I am all they have for hope. Without me, they are doomed.

Before I know it, I see the Command Headquarters and my loft just behind the tent.

I fly directly in, not bothering to stop on the perch outside as I enter.

The bell rings, announcing my arrival.

I collapse on the floor of the loft.

I made it. I still have the precious cargo dangling from my shattered leg. My boys will live.

A soldier comes to read the latest message from the front located in the silver canister on my leg. When he sees me with my shattered leg, blood streaming from the bullet wound, and missing eye, he gasps.

"Cher Ami, you've returned to us!" he cries out,

as he gingerly removes the message from my dangling leg.

I've done my job. I made it.

*****

On October 3, 1918, during the Argonne Offensive, Major Charles White Whittlesey was trapped with 500 men in a small depression on the side of a hill behind enemy lines with little food or ammunition. They were under constant enemy fire, while also receiving fire from allied artillery who did not know their location. Surrounded by the Germans, many were killed and wounded in the first day and by the second day, more than half of the unit was injured or killed. Whittlesey had three carrier pigeons at his disposal to dispatch messages, but the first and second pigeons were shot down by the Germans before they could make it off the battlefield. Only one homing pigeon was left: "Cher Ami." She was dispatched with a note in a canister on her left leg, "We are along the road parallel to 276.4. Our own artillery is dropping a barrage directly on us. For heaven's sake, stop it."

As Cher Ami took off, she was immediately fired upon by the surrounding Germans. She flew through the unrelenting fire until she was hit and fell to the ground. After a few moments she took flight again, evacuating the battlefield and returning to her loft with her precious cargo in the silver canister attached to her now shattered leg. When she arrived back at her loft at division headquarters 25 miles to the rear in just 25 minutes, she was found to have been shot through the heart, missing one eye, and her leg with the message on it was hanging by a tendon. Despite her injury, her mission was a success. The message she carried helped save the lives of 194 men from her unit.

Cher Ami became the hero of the 77th Infantry Division. Army medics endeavored to save her life, but they could not save her leg. They then carved a small wooden one for her. When she recovered enough to travel, the now one-legged bird was put on a boat to the United States, with General John J. Pershing personally seeing Cher Ami off as she departed France.

Cher Ami (French masculine for Dear Friend) was one of approximately 600 homing pigeons donated to the U.S. Army Signal Corps by the pigeon fanciers of Britain. Originally assumed to be male, Cher Ami turned out to be a female pigeon. Upon arriving in the United States, Cher Ami was awarded the Croix de Guerre Medal with a palm Oak Leaf Cluster, for her heroic service in delivering 12 important messages in Verdun. She also received the Silver Star from General Pershing. She died at Fort Monmouth, New Jersey, on June 13, 1919 from the wounds she received in battle. Cher Ami was later inducted into the Racing Pigeon Hall of Fame in 1931. She also received a gold medal from the Organized Bodies of American Racing Pigeon Fanciers in recognition of her extraordinary service during World War I.

Cher Ami as displayed in the Smithsonian Museum

Cher Ami is not the only animal recognized for gallantry, or even the only pigeon. Many animals have given their lives in sacrifice to human wars. The United Kingdom recognizes these animals through the Dickin Medal, of which there are 32 pigeon recipients from World War II alone.

To American schoolchildren of the 1920s and 1930s, Cher Ami was as well-known as any human World War I heroes. Cher Ami's body was later mounted by a taxidermist and enshrined in the Smithsonian Institution. It is currently on display with that of Sergeant Stubby, official mascot of 102nd Infantry Regiment, in the National Museum of American History's *Price of Freedom* exhibit.

Child of Ice

"Quiet, he'll hear us," my brother whispers with his authoritative tone.

"I am being quiet, you be quiet!" I snark back as I duck under the window to be on the same side as Halidor.

Peering through the bottom corner of the window, I can make out one of the green men standing before the counter.

"What do you see?" Hali asks.

Always relying on me to be his eyes and ears.

He probably doesn't want to put his big head in the window, giving us away to the invaders.

"He's cutting potatoes," I whisper in Hali's red ear.

"Andri, get a better look, he's up to something." Hali sternly whispers back.

Why are you always ordering me to do what you are too afraid to do, you big oaf?

I look up through the window again, this time catching the green man with short-cropped hair and a look of efficiency mixed with longing as he drops the sliced potatoes into a frying pan.

What, frying . . . potatoes?

"He's frying potatoes!" I laugh, a little too loud.

Grabbing my arm, Hali yanks me as he orders, "Let's go, let's go!"

That hurts!

"Hali, that hurts! Let go!" I scream out.

Hali doesn't let go, but drags me back toward our house.

"Let go Hali, let go of me!" I scream.

"Hali, take your hands off your brother!" Mama calls out from our front door.

Oh Mama. Thank you.

"Mama, Mama . . ." Hali screams as he runs up to our door. "Mama, the green man was frying potatoes!"

Mama runs her right hand through Hali's blond hair as I catch up to clutch mama's left hand.

"Now boys, don't be spying on our guests. You know better than that," she says in the stern voice she uses when talking to both of us at once.

I hug Mama's hand.

Comfort at the familiar.

Hali looks up at her face as she lowers her eyes at him.

"What nonsense," she said. "Nobody would fry potatoes, you must not have seen right. We fry kleinur and parta, but not potatoes!"

I knew it, those green "guests" are strange.

Hali glares at me, a look of pending retribution in his eyes.

Ha, I told the truth, and it still made you say something almost as stupid as you look!

*****

On May 10, 1940, the British invaded Iceland to ensure it not fall under German control. The Prime Minister of Iceland, knowing he could not stop the invasion, broadcast to his people to invite the British in, treating them as guests in their homes. The British soldiers then took up residence in homes throughout the country.

In one occurrence, two boys were spying on a British soldier making his meal when they spotted him frying potatoes. They could not believe it. No one in Iceland had ever heard of frying potatoes. When they returned home they told their mother, who did not believe anyone would fry a potato. Only years later did one of the little boys come to the United States and order a burger and fries without knowing what it was. He found out fried potatoes are very good indeed. You think he called his mother?

Stonne

"AP!" I yell.

Krause removes an armor piercing shell from the wicker basket, handing it to Fuchs, the loader.

Fuchs places the AP round gently within the open breach on our Pak-36 anti-tank gun.

Pohl closes the breach, making the gun ready.

We're dug in and loaded, ready for the inevitable French counter-attack.

"Now we wait," I tell my men, as we scan through the town and up the lane on the right.

Armor crews rush to their idling tanks, all lined up in a column up the narrow lane in the small village of Stonne.

Small French houses bracket each tank in the line.

Any of those could be my house. This could be Boppard, where Mom is now. What if the French offensive had broken through the Siegfried Line last year, advancing all the way through Boppard? What if Mom had been in a house surrounded by French tanks?

Damn those French tanks!

Just as I think about French tanks, a Char-B1 appears up the road, on the edge of this small French town.

The moment I notice it, it fires two shots; one from its 47mm turret gun, and the other from its hull-mounted 75mm gun.

He was ready!

Instantly, the first and last tanks in the column lined up on that narrow street burst into flames.

Get him, Get him!

"Prepare to fire at that Char-B if he comes within range," I calmly tell my crew.

We all stare in amazement as the French tank moves forward, rapidly firing both guns at the line of German tanks.

The German tanks fire back; all nine left in operation are pounding the French tank with everything they can throw at it.

Nothing is penetrating!

That thing is a beast!

The Char-B keeps coming, knocking down tank after tank in the German column.

Four German tanks are burning as they are pushed aside by the oncoming French monster.

"In range!" Vogt screams above the sound of more shells firing and the eruption of our compatriot's flammable armored vehicles.

"Fire!" I scream back.

At this range we're just knocking on the door.

"AP!" I yell, starting the loading process for my AT gun all over again.

The French tank simply continues forward, impervious to all the steel we throw at it.

Krause removes another armor piercing shell from the wicker basket, again handing it to Fuchs.

Our shell quietly disappears into the Char's armor, with no discernible result.

Fuchs places the AP round gently within the open breach.

Pohl closes the breach, making the gun ready.

The French tank is closer now.

May this round find its way home!

"Fire!" I scream, yet again launching an armor piercing shell at the French Char-B.

Another two Panzers explode as the Char-B thrusts its way through the small town.

"AP!" I yell, repeating the loading process.

The French tank continues forward, so it is now only a few hundred meters away.

Again, the shell is absorbed in the French tank's thick armor, with no result.

It's as if that thing is swallowing our steel, then spitting it back out at our tanks as it goes.

Krause removes one more armor piercing shell from the wicker basket, handing it to Fuchs.

Fuchs places the AP round gently within the open breach.

Pohl closes the breach, making the gun ready.

Our tanks rapidly fire at the onrushing French machine, but their shots are as ineffective as my own.

Another two Panzers explode.

How many are dying from this one French Char-B?

I sure hope he's alone!

"AP!" I yell, hoping the closing range will help my rounds penetrate.

Krause slowly removes an armor piercing shell from the wicker basket, as he stares at the oncoming French beast.

Fuchs reaches out, taking the shell from Krause.

Their faces are solid with fear.

Is my face expressing the same thing?

That monster is under 100 meters away and still coming strong.

"Stay focused on your duty," I remind my crew.

Their faces turn back to their work.

Fuchs places the AP round gently within the open breach.

Pohl sternly closes the breach, prepping the gun.

"Fire!" I yell just as two more Panzers blow up.

That's the last of our tanks.

Now it's up to us.

The French tank dashes toward us.

Our last round ricocheting off the front armor plate.

We're useless against this behemoth!

As he closes range, we should penetrate.

We should!

"AP!" I scream, knowing this will be our last round before he's on us.

The French tank's machine gun opens on us, spitting rounds all around our position.

This is it!

Krause removes an armor piercing shell from the wicker basket, while his body trembles.

"Krause, stay with us."

A round smashes through Krause's left leg, crumpling him just as he hands the round to Fuchs, whose face is pale white.

"This is our last chance to knock it down. Load up Fuchs!" I scream.

Fuchs automatically places the round in the breach, which Pohl snaps shut.

They are breaking!

"Medic! Medic!" Fuchs screams, hoping to help Krause.

Am I breaking?

"Fire!" I scream, as I stare down the on-rushing

French monster.

"NOTHING!" I holler before realizing anything slipped out.

Krause is writing in agony on the ground with Fuchs over him.

We're no longer an operational unit.

BCHCHCHOOOOO

I'm blown away from my gun.

Darkness surrounds my small area of remaining sight.

That Monster bit me too!

Looking back toward where my gun had been set-up, I see Pohl dangling over the destroyed breach.

I can't see Fuchs or Krause anywhere.

The French tank has already turned, making its way up the small lane to our right.

Hopefully the other Pak-36 over there can find a way to penetrate his armor.

My eyes go dark.

My world goes quiet.

My mind goes still.

*****

French Char B-1

On May 16, 1940, a single French B1 named *Eure* and commanded by Captain Billotte, forced its way into the town of Stonne. Hotly contested, Stonne switched sides 17 times over the course of the German invasion of France. Captain Billotte's Eure attacked a German column from Panzer Regiment 8, destroying two Panzer IV and 11 Panzer III tanks, along with two Pack-36 anti-tank guns. After his successful assault, Captain Billotte turned around, heading back out of the village. His tank had endured 140 shell impacts, all of which failed to penetrate the thick armor of this massive beast of a machine. After the battle, Billotte was nicknamed *The Butcher of*

Stonne.

Contrary to popular opinion, even though France eventually fell to the German onslaught, the French put up a heck of a fight with some advanced and awesomely powerful equipment. Poor communication, tactics, and strategic leadership, as well as operational plans and some good German luck led to France's defeat. Still, despite their fall, they were able to inflict heavy losses on the Germans.

Today Captain Billotte's Eure can be seen in the center of Stonne. His name is also given to an award in the game *World of Tanks* in which the player destroys many enemy vehicles quickly. Pierre Armand Gaston Billotte went on to serve as a military attaché, a division commander, the head of France's military mission to the United Nations, and eventually Minister of National Defense.

Payback

Plexiglas separates my bent frame from the receding coastline below as we head north into the Babuyan Channel toward the Luzon Straits.

I hope we find some Japs!

Scanning the horizon ahead takes my mind off the reason for this mission, but not for long.

Payback!

My eyes dart from west to east, searching for ships heading south toward the Philippines. For all eight of us, payback can't be pushed out of our heads by any activity, especially one as mundane as searching the horizon.

Despite having the best view in the plane, I can't see beyond the cloud cover on this overcast December day.

Payback for the attack going on at Clark Field right now that forced us to scramble into the sky only partially loaded, Payback for Pearl Harbor, payback for starting this damn war!

"Smoke at 11 o'clock," Bean yells on the communication system.

Damn, I wanted to be the one to spot it! How'd I miss the smoke?

I swing my head back toward the west again, seeing a small dark plume rising from the water.

"Adjusting our heading to target it," Captain Kelly informs the crew.

We're out for blood!

Theirs, and probably ours, as we're also out here alone: A solo mission to bomb any target of opportunity we happen to find.

Just two days after the surprise at Clark Field caught most of our bombers and fighters on the ground, we're on a bombing mission to slow down the expected Japanese invasion of the Philippines.

"That's a big one!" hollers Robbins, the co-pilot.

Eying the smoke stack, I can discern an outline of a large ship steaming south as part of a group of vessels.

They can only be Japs. We don't have anything

that big out here!

"**Targeting the big one, got that Levin?**" Cap informs me.

YES!

"**Roger Captain, targeting the big one,**" I reply.

Our distance should be about seven miles, give or take.

I've had the Norden bombsight's gyros running since shortly after takeoff. The computer is all warmed up. Clutching in the stabilizer, my right hand grips both the turn and drift knobs, rotating them to change the heading of the plane toward the ship.

"**Adjusting heading, Levin. Take it easy on that computer!**" Cap calls out.

What does he expect? This is our first combat mission, and he wants me to take it easy!

"**Yes, Cap,**" I reply.

Engaging the telescope motor clutch, I lower my right eye to the bombsights eyepiece, using my right hand to adjust the angle so the ship shows up in the cross-hairs of the scope.

Steady.

Too much angle and I overshoot the ship.

Must rotate the stabilizers back.

Clutching the vertical stabilizers, I uncage the gyros, allowing the site to track the ship.

Drifting left, away from the target.

Correcting for the drift, I double grip the turn and drift knobs again, gently nudging them forward.

Yes, on target now, but coming in fast. Oh wait, the bomb-bay doors.

With my right hand, I flip the bay doors switch, exposing our three 600-pound bombs to the world below.

Slowly turning the rate motor switch, I reduce the rate at which the plane is approaching the target.

Alright, the cross-hairs are steady on the target.

I level up by turning the leveling knob with my left hand so the scope is aligned and both bubbles are centered.

My reference is vertical, yes!

Eye back to the eyepiece, the target has drifted away from the cross-hairs. Right hand on the vertical stabilizers, I correct with the drift knobs one more time, flipping the automatic release lever.

No more corrections now, let's see what this computer can do!

"Computer's got the target, Cap!" I report.

"Going steady then," Cap Kelly retorts.

The moments tick by as our aircraft approaches the sky above the large ship. At 22,000 feet, I can't make out much on the ship itself, but it's a big one, that's for sure!

Staring down at it, I wonder:

Do they even know we're up here?

After a pause between thoughts, the plane rises with the wind to the east, catching more air because of reduced weight.

"Bombs Away!" I call out, excitedly.

"Turning off auto-pilot," I follow, in a less enthusiastic manner.

I kinda miss controlling the plane.

My eyes stay on the large ship below. Small bursts of fire erupt from guns on its deck.

They've spotted us and are firing back.

A large explosion erupts at the stern of the ship sending a plume of flame skyward.

"YES! A HIT!" I scream into the coms.

"Great job Levin, but hold off on the hollering will ya!" Robbins, the co-pilot, requests.

"Let's get this bird home," Cap suggests.

"Splash one Jap Battleship!" Halkyard bellows from the waist-guns.

"One less battlewagon for you Japs! Ha!" Money calls out.

Captain Kelly turns our B-17 so we're heading back toward Luzon and Clark Field.

Payback feels good!

*****

B-17 Bomber

December 10, 1941 a lone U.S. Army Air Corps
B-17 bomber out of Clark Field in the Philippines
successfully targeted a large Japanese ship north of
Luzon, initially believed to be the battleship *Haruna.*
The ship burst into flames while the crew of the
bomber turned to head back to its base. Captain Kelly
reported a major sinking. This news was a huge boost
of sorely needed good news just days after the attack
on Pearl Harbor and the destruction of most Air
Corps planes in the Philippines the next morning. For
the sake of truth, there were no battleships in the area
that day, and the plane slightly damaged the Japanese

cruiser *Natori* when the ship was hit with a single 600-pound bomb.

Time Life Books *The Rising Sun,* 1977, page 91.

http://img834.image-shack.us/img834/9351/boeingb17cflyingfortres.jpg - graphic of early model B-17 (likely in Philippines)

http://www.stelzriede.com/ms/photos/b17d.jpg - great pic of early model B-17

Kelly

Let's get out of here!

Banking the giant B-17 170 degrees starboard, I put us on a new heading (south by south-east) so we're in line with Clark Field.

Just as I finish the turn, Money in the top turret calls out, **"Fighters 5 o'clock high!"**

"Altman, before you get in the bathtub, let Clark know we splashed a battleship!" I order to our radio operator.

"Yes, Cap" he replies.

From multiple points behind the cockpit, the staccato cracks of machine guns clatter as hammers strike the rear end of belted shells, propelling each explosive projectile toward the incoming Jap Zeroes.

Robbins turns his head to look out over his right shoulder toward the incoming flight of Japs, "A whole swarm of 'em! This is going to get ugly."

We hit that ship on a mission that might never have happened, so we're already ahead.

Despite the on-rushing enemy machine gun and

cannon shells tearing through the thin skin of my lumbering giant bird, my glove-covered hands steady the vibrations, keeping trim and level flight.

Now we'll see how much of a flying fortress this bird really is.

Shearing metal, human screams, staccato shell impacts, whizzing streaks of near-missed rounds, and blood-curdling shrieks of plane fragments torn away from the man-made contraption holding me aloft combine to crescendo into a cacophony of impulse overload silence.

Keep the plane flying, just fly the damn plane.

"Delehanty's down, he's bleeding," someone yells into the coms in a voice too excited to be identified.

"You get Delehanty, I'll cover your gun," Bean offers over the coms.

He must be talking to the new guy, waist gunner Altman.

"Take out the one with the yellow stripe" Sergeant Altman, now in the bathtub turret, orders in a confident voice, perfectly calm, as if he is walking along a beach rather than fighting for his life and that of our plane.

Two Robert Altmans on my crew, what were the odds?

Keep it steady and fly the plane.

"Where's the stripe?" Money asks.

"7, he's at 7 High," Halkyard, the other waist gunner, replies.

"Got 'em. Take care of 4 Level," Money calls out.

"He's going too fast for me," Halkyard grudgingly concedes.

"I got 3 low," Altman offers from the tub.

"Whoa, did you see him go by?" Money asks no one in particular.

"Shut it, only use coms to call them out." Robbins pipes in, attempting to keep the coms clear for the gunners.

"Engine 2's hit, CATCHING FIRE!" Money shrieks into the coms.

Shit, a fire in 2. We can still make it back if the fuel doesn't catch.

"I'm shutting down the fuel to 2 and feathering the props," Robbins tells me, not looking in my direction.

"They're breaking off," Levin calls out from the nose.

"How's Delehanty?" I ask, hoping new Altman's got him covered.

Silence.

"Atman, how's Delehanty?" Money chimes in.

"Money, get down there and check on Delehanty and Altman," Robbins orders.

After a few moments of silence, Money comes back on the coms, ***"Delehanty's dead, Altman's bleeding Cap."***

Tub Altman comes on the coms, **"Engine 4's leaking, Cap. A dark stream streaking out."**

Engine 4 is leaking fuel. If the fire in 2 touches the fuel from 4, we're done for.

"Shutting down the fuel feed to 4 and feathering the props," Robbins informs me.

This bird has a good chance of exploding.

"Japs are coming back," tub Altman reports on

coms.

Summoning an air of gravitas despite my sense of dread, I order, **"EVERYONE OUT, NOW!"**

"I MEAN IT, JUMP NOW!"

Turning right so my vision is in line with Robbins, I order, "YOU TOO!"

"Someone break me out of here," tub Altman orders more than requests.

I can't imagine being stuck in the ball turret, dependent upon someone else in the plane to open the door for me.

Keep her steady.

Robbins starts to get up from his co-pilot seat, pauses for a moment while looking at me, puts his hand on my shoulder, and says, "Level it off and get out too."

"I will."

He folds himself in half, disappearing through the bulkhead.

My hands tremble in rhythm with the jittering plane.

Hold it together girl, we'll get you home.

A Jap Zero streaks past so close I can see the pilots face.

Keep it steady.

The plane, despite its now violent vibrations, is staying level and steady, offering a perfect jumping platform for my crew.

I flip the switch to engage the autopilot, but when I let go of the steering column the wings bank slightly to port.

If the autopilot doesn't work, I can't get to an exit fast enough before this bird flips over and starts spinning.

One engine on each side, with two feathered, if I put them in sync, even though they are not parallel, they could keep the bird stable.

I reduce the power to Engine 3, so that 1 is dominant.

Ok, that should do it.

Engaging the auto-pilot again, I pause for a moment to observe the plane.

Steady and stable, great!

Lifting myself from the Captain's seat, my eye

catches an incoming fighter at 3 O'clock, fiery bursts streaming from behind his prop.

Get out!

*****

Returning from what they believed to be a successful bombing run against a Japanese battleship, the crew of Captain Colin Kelly's B-17(c) was jumped by a squadron of Japanese Zero fighters commanded by one of Japan's most vaunted aces of the war, Saburo Sakai. Captain Kelly held the plane steady long enough for his six surviving crew members to escape before (and sources differ here) it either blew up or crashed. The Japanese fighter pilots could not definitively report which occurred, so a probable kill was split between several members of the squadron. This B-17 was the first American bomber lost in actual combat in World War II. Captain Kelly, a graduate of West Point, died in the loss.

The Legend of Colin Kelly by Robert Taylor

The crew that day were:

Pilot Captain Colin Purdie Kelly, Jr. (KIA, BR) Madison, FL

Co-Pilot 2nd Lt. Donald Robbins (survived)

Navigator 2nd Lt. Joe M. Bean (survived)

Bombardier Cpl Meyer Levin, 6975479 (survived) NY

Engineer SSgt William J. Delehanty (KIA, BR) NY

Radio/Bathtub Gunner Pfc Robert E. Altman (survived)

Assistant Radio/Gunner Willard Money (survived)

Gunner Pvt Robert Altman (WIA)

Waist Gunner SSgt James Halkyard (survived)

In the haste to share a small victory with a depressed military and civilian populace still reeling from the attack on Pearl Harbor and the surprise destruction of the U.S. air units at Clark Field the next day, the details of Kelly's sacrifice were confused and exaggerated. Reports of him crashing the bomber into a Japanese battleship, together with other equally false claims, encouraged many Americans to believe he was the first American suicide pilot of the war and deserved to be awarded The Medal of Honor. Kelly was a hero for saving his crew on America's first bombing mission of World War II. He received the Distinguished Service Cross, the nation's second highest award for heroism, both for the assumed damage or destruction of the Japanese battleship *Haruna* but, especially, for the persona sacrifice which saved his crew.

Captain Kelly is considered the first American hero of World War II. Several streets, schools, post offices, and monuments around the country bear his name. His remains are buried in Madison, Florida (his hometown), and a statue in his honor resides in Four Freedoms Park. Kelly was survived by a small child, Colin B. *"Corky "* Kelley III. A nation-wide effort, spearheaded by a Tampa newspaper, raised thousands of dollars for a *Corky* fund to help care for the child. President Roosevelt penned a request to *the President of the United States in 1956*. In the letter, F.D.R. asked that the airman's infant son get a West

Point appointment. Colin Kelly III did attend and graduate from West Point, eventually becoming a priest and serving as an Assistant Chaplain at West Point.

Table It

Pulling out the paper on the invasion of mainland Europe, I place it on the table before me.

This is what they came for.

"The British Chief of Staff's Committee would like to table the paper on the topic of invading mainland Europe," I announce to the Combined Chiefs of Staff Committee.

Half the room, only the Americans, erupt in surprise and disappointment.

"What do you mean table it?" General Marshall, the Chief of Staff of the United States Army replies, representing the American side.

I thought they'd want us to talk about this. It is their bailiwick, after all.

"Yes, we'd like to table the motion of invading mainland Europe in 1942," I repeat.

They may have simply misunderstood me the first time.

"We can't table that," General Marshall retorts almost instantly. "That is the primary topic we came to discuss."

Of course, it's what we all came to discuss. That's why we brought it up. Why are they fighting it?

The entire American delegation huddles together: Chief of Staff of the Army, Chief of Naval Operations, Chief of the Army Air Corps, (*Why is their air service part of their Army?*) and the Secretaries of their Army and Navy. So much brass and pinstripes on their side, one would almost feel sorry for the marching band from which they must have pilfered it all.

"The invasion of mainland Europe is of prime importance to our side. We must insist it not be tabled now. Otherwise, we have nothing further to discuss today," General Marshall announces in a commanding, yet gentle, voice.

If it's so important to you, and us, then why must we not table it now?

"Yes, the invasion of mainland Europe is of prime importance to our side as well, which is the very reason we wish to table it now. There are other topics which can wait until we address this one," I reply, still not understanding the American's insistence to prevent it from being discussed.

"We have to discuss it now!" demands General Marshall, putting a fist to the table to emphasize his point as his entourage backs him by standing in a cluster behind.

You cannot order us to do something we want to do anyway!

"Perhaps I may offer a point of clarification," Air Marshall Harris chimes in.

"It appears to me both sides wish to discuss the invasion of mainland Europe. Is this correct?" the Air Marshall asks the room.

"Yes, that is correct," General Marshall replies instantly, revealing a consternation not often seen with such a rank.

"Yes, right then," Harris quickly retorts.

You've got it Harris, that's it!

"Then perhaps we are on the same page, and simply the definition of 'Table It' is what's ruffling the matter," Harris offers.

Slowly the American delegation retakes their seats.

"So, we'll discuss the invasion of mainland Europe next then?" General Marshall asks.

"If by next you mean now, then yes," I reply. "For us, next means after what we're doing right now."

General Marshall looks at me.

General Arnold of the United States Army Air Corps slams a cigar on the table.

Major General Thomas Holcomb, Commandant of the United States Marine Corps, slams his fist in a laugh.

"Gentlemen, may we proceed with discussing the invasion of Mainland Europe?" I ask.

In unison, the room erupts. "YES!"

"Let's proceed," I declare.

*****

Allied Combined Chiefs of Staff

Turns out the same words don't always mean the same thing. During the Second World War, the British and Americans came together at multiple conferences to plan the conduct of the war. One of the first, ARCADIA, took place from late 1941 through early 1942 and formed the foundation of the British American Alliance, which persists to this day. Yet, at that conference, not everything went as smoothly as it could. Here is a quote from Winston Churchill discussing the event:

The enjoyment of a common language was of

course a supreme advantage in all British and American discussions. The delays and often partial misunderstandings, which occur when interpreters are used, were avoided. There was however, differences of expression, which in the early days led to an amusing incident. The British Staff prepared a paper, which they wished to raise as a matter of urgency, and informed their American colleagues that they wished to "table it." To the American Staff, "tabling" a paper, meant putting it away in a drawer and forgetting it. A long and even acrimonious argument ensued before both parties realized that they were agreed on the merits and wanted the same thing.

Zoot

"**A**in't nothing here but some two-bit singers," Lafferty reports while exiting another dive.

"I want a burger," Jenkins cries as he walks behind Lafferty.

I just want to eat something, don't matter what it is.

"Come on guys; let's head down the block toward the market. We can pick up some chow there," I suggest.

As I finish the phrase, a couple of Pachucos sporting zoot suits come 'round the corner.

Lafferty turns, tapping Jenkins on the shoulder to get his attention.

Jenkins darts in front of the Pachucos, his uniform flowing as the air catches it when he lands.

"Hey muchacho," Jenkins calls out to the surprised Pachucos. "Why you help'n out the Japs?"

The center Pachuco turns his head left, making eye contact with one of his buddies.

"Come on Jenkins, let's get some chow," I call

out, moving in behind him.

Jenkins turns to me, while blocking the Pachuco's path.

"They're wast'en, while good Amer'cans savin'. We can't let 'em be wastin' n' more!"

Lafferty pulls up beside me, so all three of us are now blocking the Pachucos.

"We ain't wast'in; we lookin' good," the Pachuco on the right counters Lafferty.

We didn't come here to fight.

With my right hand, I grab Jenkins' right shoulder; with my left, I push his left shoulder, spinning him toward me.

"We're hungry. Let's eat," I say.

Lafferty turns his head toward me.

The Pachucos walk on, moving around us as they go.

With his left, Jenkins grabs my hand, twirling me about so my right shoulder brushes the back of the so far silent Pachuco's jacket.

Damn Jenkins!

The Pachuco taps his buddy while turning toward

me, his left arm raised high.

Jenkins, who's faster than me, blocks the Pachuco's arm, while delivering an uppercut into his soft belly.

Collapsing from the blow, the Pachuco screams out.

Now we started something.

The other two Pachucos grab their buddy, lifting him up, while turning to face the three of us.

Bouncing on the balls of his feet, Jenkins is looking for a fight. He calls out, "That'll teach you to waste so much! It's Un'merican!"

Lafferty gets himself into a fighting stance.

Do I fight?

Once he's standing on his own again, the two other Pachucos pull their friend with them, attempting to turn to head back the way they came.

Jenkins runs up after them, Lafferty at his side.

I don't want to fight these guys, I want to eat.

Jenkins pulls the Pachuco on the left back by the collar of his jacket, throwing him to the ground.

Lafferty does the same to the Pachuco on the

right.

Both men start kicking the guys. Kicking hard.

"Hey, stop kicking them, we were going for chow!" I yell out as I run up on 'em.

As I make it to their sides, Jenkins bends down and starts pulling the zoot suit jacket off his Pachuco.

Lafferty sees Jenkins doing this, so he starts in on his.

Screaming, flailing with their arms, and kicking with their feet, the Pachucos try to resist, but eight weeks of basic training and drill have made Jenkins and Lafferty too strong for these soft city rats.

I look away, not wanting to witness my friends beating anyone.

Why did they have to waste so much fabric on their clothes?

My knees get week. I reach out to hold on to the wall of a building.

Just as I touch the building, two patrolmen come around the corner.

I turn again toward Jenkins, who is now urinating on the jacket he ripped off the Pachuco.

Lafferty is doing the same thing.

Walk away, just walk away.

The patrolmen pull out their batons.

Jenkins calls out, "Hey, these Pachucos are Jap agents!"

Without looking at each other, the patrolmen start hammering blows with their batons onto the two hapless Pachucos.

The third starts to run.

One of the patrol officers turns and starts chasing after him.

The Pachuco is too fast for the officer, who gives up, returning to rain more blows of his baton down on the helpless man on the ground.

Jenkins and Lafferty zip up.

Turning to me, Jenkins announces, "I'm starvin'. Let's get that chow."

Lafferty replies, "Yeah, I could eat a horse!"

I'm not hungry anymore.

*****

A series of conflicts erupted in Los Angeles between U.S. servicemen and Mexican-American youths in June 1943. The youths wore broad-shouldered jackets, balloon-leg trousers, and very large hats, sometimes with feathers. These outfits were called Zoot Suits. Those who wore these outfits referred to themselves as Pachucos, a label connected with a rebellion against both Mexican and American values and cultures.

During the violence, white servicemen and civilians attacked and stripped the Pachucos, claiming they considered the outfits unpatriotic during wartime, as they used too much rationed fabric. While most of the violence was directed toward Mexican

American youth, young African-Americans and Fil-
ipino-Americans who were wearing zoot suits were
also attacked.

The riots began on June 3, 1943, after a group of
sailors claimed they had been attacked by a group of
Mexican-American zoot-suiters. On June 4, many
uniformed sailors chartered cabs to Mexican-American communities, seeking out the zoot-suiters. Many
zoot-suiters were beaten by servicemen and stripped
of their zoot suits on the spot. The servicemen sometimes urinated on the zoot suits or burned them in the
streets. One local paper printed an article describing
how to de-zoot a zoot-suiter, including directions
that the zoot suits should be burned. The servicemen

were also portrayed in local news publications as heroes fighting against what was referred to as a Mexican crime wave. The worst of the fighting occurred on the night of June 7, when thousands of servicemen and citizens prowled the streets of downtown Los Angeles, attacking zoot-suiters as well as members of minority groups who were not wearing zoot suits.

In response to these confrontations, police arrested hundreds of Mexican-American youths, many of whom had already been attacked by servicemen. There were also reports of Mexican-American youths requesting to be arrested and locked up to protect themselves from the servicemen in the streets. In contrast, very few sailors and soldiers were arrested during the riots.

Shortly after midnight on June 8, military officials declared Los Angeles off-limits to all military personnel. Deciding the local police were completely unable or unwilling to handle the situation, the military ordered military police to patrol parts of the city and arrest disorderly military personnel. The next day the Los Angeles City Council passed a resolution banning the wearing of zoot suits on Los Angeles streets. The number of attacks dwindled, largely ending by June 10. In the following weeks, however, similar disturbances occurred in other states.

No one was killed during the riots, although many people were injured. Considerably more Mexican-Americans than servicemen were arrested, fueling criticism of the Los Angeles Police Department's response to the riots.

As the riots died down, California Gov. Earl Warren (a future Supreme Court Chief Justice) ordered the creation of a citizens' committee to investigate and determine the cause of the Zoot Suit Riots. The committee's report indicated several factors involved, with racism the central cause of the riots, exacerbated by the response of the Los Angeles Police Department as well as by biased and inflammatory media coverage. Los Angeles Mayor Fletcher Bowron, concerned about the riots' negative impact on the city's image, issued his own conclusion, stating racial prejudice was not a factor and the riots were caused by juvenile delinquents.

A week after the riots, First Lady Eleanor Roosevelt commented on them in her newspaper column. "The question goes deeper than just suits. It is a racial protest. I have been worried for a long time about the Mexican racial situation. It is a problem with roots going a long way back, and we do not always face these problems as we should." – June 16, 1943.

The *Los Angeles Times* published an editorial the next day expressing outrage, accusing Mrs. Roosevelt of having communist leanings and stirring race discord.

On June 21, 1943, the State Un-American Activities Committee, under State Senator Jack Tenney, arrived in Los Angeles with orders to "determine whether the present Zoot Suit Riots were sponsored by Nazi agencies attempting to spread disunity between the United States and Latin-American countries." Although Tenney claimed he had evidence the riots were Axis-sponsored, no evidence was ever presented to support this claim.

The events did, though, serve as a propaganda tool against the United States. Japanese media broadcasts accused the United States' government of ignoring the brutality of U.S. Marines toward Mexicans.

Birthday

*T*hey are all here!

Every one of my children, grandchildren, and great-grandchildren pack the dining area of Ben's Deli in Manhattan.

How Otto could reserve the whole restaurant, I don't know.

"How did you do it, bringing us all together?" I ask my first son.

"Ma, we've been planning this for a while. Everyone said yes right away," Otto replies.

Named after the grandfather he never met, my son's eyes are the same deep brown as my father's.

I sit in the center of the room, a blanket wrapped over my legs.

My children, grandchildren, and many incredibly energetic great-grandchildren whirl throughout the large mirror-walled room.

How many are even here? I can't count them all.

What energy. What life. What joy!

"Happy Birthday, Grandma!" Margot, my

youngest grandchild, calls out as she softly takes hold of my hand.

Her pre-college schoolgirl look reminds me of my older sister Margot before we left Amsterdam.

We were lucky to end up in the United States.

Laughter, cake, and more cake energize the room.

I look over the gathering, seeing smiling faces, humor, and love. I see artists, lawyers, doctors, even writers like me. Engineers, mechanics, songwriters, a movie director, actors, and a Congresswoman all in one room, all from my family.

Who would have known such a story could unfold? A German girl, evacuated to the Netherlands, then again to the United States within such a short time, finding love, starting a family, building a career focused on life and art, raising such children.

Turning toward Mark, I can't help but cry.

He reaches out to me, his frail arms warmly wrapping around my body as they have for more than fifty years.

"Thank you," he whispers in my ear.

"Me, I didn't do anything," I reply.

"Just being born, and then agreeing to be my wife. Just being here," he declares.

Just being here.

*****

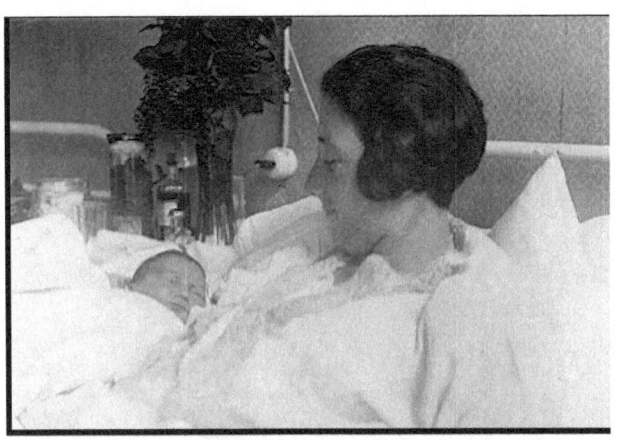

Anne Frank's father, Otto Frank, attempted to immigrate to the United States shortly after the family fled Germany for Holland. Here is an article describing the reason the family was unable to make that trip. (http://historybuff.com/anne-frank-was-a-refugee-who-was-denied-entrance-to-the-united-states-MWVgqxJLAjJ2) This story asks you to imagine if Otto Frank had been successful in this bid to escape Hitler's hate and Europe's decline into blood-soiled war and human tragedy. Below you'll see a blog post about this special day, and just one of the many millions of blessings to the world we lost because of such hate-filled anti-immigrant policies.

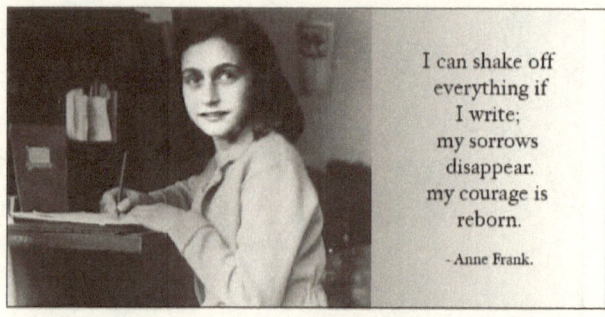

I can shake off everything if I write; my sorrows disappear. my courage is reborn.

- Anne Frank.

Let's think about today's refugee crisis. Are we condemning others to a similar fate as Anne? How many future birthdays are being lost because of our inaction?

Oops

A kill!

Going down with flame and black smoke trailing from the engines and across the left wing, his Spitfire plummets toward the body of water.

That was a good pilot.

Watching the plane as it descends in a smoking twirl toward the sea, I see the pilot emerge with a parachute.

Good he'll make it.

I've got to get out of here!

As I pause a moment to reassess my position, I check the fuel gauge. I'm not surprised, but forlorn, to see it teetering near empty.

Where did I end up? How do I get back to a friendly field from here?

I scan the horizon, taking in any landmarks I can use to navigate.

A channel of water rests calmly below me.

Ah, the Channel. I just need to cross that, and I'll be home.

Banking the FW-190, the newest and most advanced aircraft in the Luftwaffe, I line up perpendicular to the channel.

Off in the distance I see an airfield, sprawling before the horizon.

Let's end this day with a little celebration.

I bank my nimble fighter toward the airfield, wagging my wings in a celebratory greeting as I approach.

Strange, no reply from the tower or any of the ground crew.

Where are the other planes on the field?

Slowly descending toward the grass strip, I can't help but wonder about the field.

Doesn't look right.

I wish I had more fuel.

Bumping along the field, I halt near a small building just as a man approaches my plane.

Why does he have a firearm?

He climbs on the wing of my fighter, approaching the cockpit.

This isn't right.

"Open up!" he demands.

English! This is an English airfield!

What have I done?

"Welcome to Blighty, Fritz, and thanks for the plane," he says as he points a flare gun at me with his right hand, removing my sidearm with his left.

I stand up from my seat. My exhausted muscles scream at the stretch of my body.

Nothing I can do about this. No fuel. No sidearm. No choice.

"Thank you for the warm greeting," I reply in broken English.

He looks at me, a bit surprised, "Well, what do you know."

He smiles at me. I smile at him, and we both climb down from what will now likely not be my fighter.

Was fun flying it while I could. What a great plane!

*****

On June 23, 1942 Oberleutnant Armin Faber, a Luftwaffe pilot, mistook the Bristol Channel for the English Channel and landed his Focke-Wulf 190 intact at RAF Pembrey in South Wales. His plane was the first FW 190 to be captured by the Allies and was tested to reveal any weaknesses that could be exploited.

Observers on the ground could not believe their eyes as Faber waggled his wings in a victory celebration, lowered the Focke-Wulf's undercarriage and landed at the field. The Pembrey Duty Pilot, Sergeant Jeffreys, identified the aircraft as German while it was landing, ordering his men to signal it to park in the dispersal area. As the FW 190 slowed, Jeffreys jumped onto its wing, taking Faber prisoner with a flare gun (as Pembrey was a training station, Jeffreys had no other weapon on hand).

Tease

Perky little sandy blond. Even in a dirty shirt and torn pants, you can tell a looker when you see one.

She strolls into the large room, confident and carefree.

Wow, what a soft face. Hazel eyes. She's gorgeous.

She sees me looking.

She looks back.

Contact!

Game On.

I look away, not wanting to seem too interested.

She looks away as well, as she brings her right hand slowly up her thigh, as she turns to reveal a nicely shaped silhouette.

Oh, you're friendly.

Her eyes locked on me now as she lifts her back leg a bit while bending slightly at the hips to push out her chest.

I'm going to enjoy this!

Adjusting my stance to accommodate some personal changes, I cut the fine figure in my *Hugo Boss* and leather boots.

Throwing her head back, she begins swinging her hips as she pulls the hem of her shirt out from her pants.

She looks as soft as the little one I had last week, but far more playful!

Slowly, and with intent, her hands rub the shirt fabric up, against her skin, revealing a pale, but tight stomach.

Show me what you got honey!

Pushing it ever higher, her shirt barely reveals the strap of a red bra before falling loosely about her torso.

She let go. Ugh.

Her eyes lock with mine again, this time just as she places her left index finger in her mouth, licks it with a gentle touch of her tongue before letting it slide under her chin, down her neck to her chest.

I stare back at her, leather baton in my left hand resting across my front to hide my enjoyment of this little show.

Swishing her hips again, she places both hands on the hem of her shirt, ripping it up and over her head in one fluid motion.

I want her!

I start toward her.

Damn the rest, this one's mine!

She crumples up her shirt, throwing it in my face.

Sweaty, grimy, dirty, female pheromones; I'm taking her right now!

Her shirt covers my face, enveloping my senses in the dream of sensuality.

Just then, I feel a shove against my chest and a grab at my right arm.

What was that?

Who was that?

Was that her?

Instead of pulling the siren shirt from my face, I reach down, unclasping my Luger from its leather holster.

What's happening?

Two hands throw my right arm up, away from

my pistol.

With my left hand, I pull the encapsulating shirt away from my face.

Dirty blond is directly before me, my pistol in her right hand.

No!

I bring my left hand up to throw the shirt in her face just as she pulls the trigger on the Luger.

PPHHUUMMPP, PPHHUUMMPP, two rounds enter my stomach.

NO! NO!

Emmerich rushes over as she turns the pistol on him, firing at his leg.

Doubling over and collapsing to the hard, cold concrete floor, I lose sight of the pretty pistol-armed inmate.

I could have had her.

Commotion reigns around me as screaming women let loose on the other guards.

It's a riot.

Automatic gunfire erupts from within the undressing room. Repetitive fire follows from outside where the rest of the prisoners were lined up waiting to enter.

We're saving gas and wasting bullets today.

I lose sight of everything.

*****

On October 23, 1943, Franceska Mann, a beautiful Polish Jew with blue-black hair was one of 1,700 Jewish women arriving at Auschwitz-Birkenau. Part of a trainload of prisoners told they were heading to Switzerland to be exchanged for German POWs, the 1,700 were told to undress before being disinfected so they could cross the border. As they were undressing, Franceska noticed SS roll call officer Josef Schillinger ogling her. There are different accounts of exactly what happened, but what is known is she seductively began to undress, keeping his attention on her. She either threw her shirt at his face or smashed a high heal against it, blocking his eyes either way. Then she grabbed his pistol, firing two shots into his stomach.

At this point, the other inmates attacked the SS guards, all of whom then rushed out of the room. Machine guns set up outside the room killed the lined-up prisoners who were waiting to enter, while grenades were thrown into the undressing room to kill those inside. Schillinger died of his wounds. Emmerich survived with a permanent disability. All 1,700 women prisoners were killed, possibly all in defiance.

The 1,700 women had been told they were a special transport, because they had all paid large amounts of money to the Gestapo for permits to immigrate to Paraguay. Turns out that was just a ruse to take their money and get them on the train. The permits were not real. Nor was the intent to send them to Switzerland. Instead, they were taken to a death camp for execution. When the women learned of this, they rose in revolt.

Also of note, the SS uniforms were made by Hugo Boss. This is how the fledgling company first came to prominence. It's done quite well since then.

Bus Ride

Turning my underpowered bus on this Kansas red dirt road, I see the next set of passengers waiting to board.

A mix of folks stand at the stop, awaiting my arrival in the dry, rust-colored summer dust.

I glide the bus to a stop, gently opening the door just as the wheels cease their rotation.

Another masterly stop.

Uniformed soldiers and made-up ladies ascend the staircase as they smile at me.

I don't want to smile. I want to drive.

They walk past me, filling in the rows behind my seat.

Reminds me of driving back in Memphis, 'cept for the roads here ain't as good.

A Negro officer and lady take seats in the second row, in front of white soldiers and ladies.

"Son, you'll have to move back," I announce to the boy, figuring the woman will move with him.

He looks at me, jaw dropping.

What, ain't no one ever talked to you like that,

nigger?

"You looking at me boy?" I say.

He don't stop lookin'.

"I am not moving. You see this uniform? You see this bar? You know what they mean? They mean I'm in the United States Army, and I'm an officer at that. You have no right to tell me to move from this seat," the boy replies.

Back home I'd haul off and slap that boy. Here, well, there's other ways to deal with the uppity.

"Have it your way, son," I reply, turning back around to finish the route.

I look back in the mirror at the Negro and his female companion, sitting in the second row.

Ain't you comfy boy?

A few more stops, we get to the end of the line. I stop the bus in another smooth glide home, parking it right in front of the base hospital.

Before the passengers have a chance to get off, I leave my seat, walk out the just-opened doors, and head over to the nearest Military Police Officer.

"Sir," I say. "I just suffered insubordination of a

young soldier on my bus. Please deal with him ac-
cordingly," as I point to the Negro who was so proud
of his little bar.

I'll show you yet, you uppity boy.

The MP walks with purpose toward the chatting
Negro, apprehending him while pushing the woman
to the side.

"You talking back, boy?" the MP says as he cuffs
the Negro.

"What are you doing? I've done nothing wrong,"
the boy protests.

"That's not what I heard, boy. You're coming
with me," the MP says as he yanks against the cuffs,
pulling the Negro soldier with him.

Ain't no Negro talkin' back to me.

*****

Jack Roosevelt Robinson became the first African-American to play in Major League Baseball (MLB) in the modern era, but this was not the first time Robinson broke a color line.

In 1942, Robinson was drafted and assigned to a segregated Army cavalry unit in Fort Riley, Kansas. Having the requisite qualifications, Robinson and several other black soldiers applied for admission to an Officer Candidate School (OCS). Although the Army's initial July 1941 guidelines for OCS had been drafted as race neutral, few black applicants

were admitted into OCS until after subsequent direc-
tives by Army leadership. As a result, the applica-
tions of Robinson and his colleagues were delayed
for several months. After protests by heavyweight
boxing champion Joe Louis (then stationed at Fort
Riley) and the help of Truman Gibson (then an assistant civilian aide to the Secretary of War), the men
were accepted into OCS. The experience led to a personal friendship between Robinson and Louis. Upon
finishing OCS, Robinson was commissioned as a
second lieutenant in January 1943.

Lt. Robinson was an officer with the 761st Tank

Battalion. This unit of African-American soldiers - later dubbed *The Black Panthers* (and *Patton's Panthers*) - became famous when they fought for 183 straight days in Europe (including at the Battle of the Bulge). Their motto was *Come Out Fighting*.

If an eventful bus ride had not sidetracked Jack Robinson during the summer of 1944, the 2nd Lieutenant could have been with his men when they shipped out to Europe and fought in Belgium later that year. Instead, he faced charges of insubordination, resulting in a court-martial.

On July 6, 1944, Robinson was awaiting results of hospital tests on the ankle he had injured in junior college. He boarded an Army bus with a fellow officer's wife. Although the Army had commissioned its own unsegregated bus line, the bus driver ordered Robinson to move to the back of the bus. Robinson refused.

The driver backed down, but after reaching the end of the line, summoned the military police, who took Robinson into custody. When Robinson later confronted the investigating duty officer about racist questioning by the officer and his assistant, the officer recommended Robinson be court-martialed. After Robinson's commander in the 761st, Paul L. Bates, refused to authorize the legal action, Robinson was summarily transferred to the 758th Battalion— where the commander quickly consented to charge Robinson with multiple offenses, including, among other charges, public drunkenness, even though Robinson did not drink.

By the time of the court-martial in August 1944, the charges against Robinson had been reduced to two counts of insubordination during questioning. Robinson was acquitted by an all-white panel of nine officers.

Desert

There he is again, slithering directly behind me.

This soldier won't leave me alone.

I scurry a little faster, hoping to lose him in the crowded street, but he keeps up, maintaining an uncomfortable distance.

I just want to get home.

His eyes, dark under the pulled down military cap, stare intently at me when I glance back to see if he's still there.

Seek help from a stranger, that is the only answer.

Reaching out to the first man I see, I plead, "Monsieur, can you please help? This soldier is following me."

Looking up, his ground-focused attention – learned through years of Nazi occupation – interrupted, the gentleman is a bit startled.

The soldier comes closer.

He's not keeping his distance any longer.

"What is the problem, Madame?" the gentleman

says, just as the soldier sidles up to tower over him.

I do not want him so close. Please help me!

"Move along, buddy," the soldier says. "My girl-friend and I are having a lover's chase, if you know what I mean."

"This soldier is not my boyfriend!" I exclaim with authority.

The gentleman is dazed, confused, and clearly wants to get away from this soldier.

Shoving the gentleman aside, the soldier turns to me, his back to the other man.

"Look here sweetheart, we're going to resolve this," he says as he grabs my hand.

"LET GO OF ME!" I scream.

The gentleman stands there, stunned.

"Help me!" I demand.

"Come with me Lucille!" the soldier projects loud enough for all to hear.

A crowd begins to gather around. The gentleman is still standing there, not knowing what to do.

"My name is not Lucille. I will not go with you. I don't know you. Let go of me!" I scream.

Yes, a lot of noise, a crowd, attention. The last things he wants!

The soldier lets go of my hand as he turns to the crowd.

"Fine, have it your way honey. I'll see you at home," he says as a parting blow to my status among the strangers in the crowd.

It worked. I am free of this monster.

"I do not know him," I plead as the crowd disperses with knowing expressions.

How dare he besmirch me near my home, this Cretin!

Scurrying home, I turn on several wrong streets to make sure the soldier is not following me.

I can't have him know where I live.

Finally turning onto my street, I see my building entrance in the distance.

Home, safety, freedom.

Making my way toward the entrance, I look around me.

The soldier is nowhere to be seen.

I walk through the outer gate, entering the front

courtyard of the building.

As I approach the front door, I look around again.

I'm not opening this door until I know I'm safe.

No one is around. I am alone.

I reach into my purse, clasping the key to the door in my right hand.

Looking up at the lock, a shadow breaks over mine on the door.

NO!

Whirling around in terror, I am prepared. The key to the door is locked between my forefinger and my middle finger.

It's not much, but it would hurt if jabbed in the eye in a quick thrust.

Thrusting my arm, I see whose shadow it is.

"Good evening, Monsieur Horbac," I say in a startled voice as I let my hand fall to my waist.

Thank god!

"Allow me to get the door, Madame," the kindly old gentleman says to me as he reaches up.

How did he surprise me?

We enter the building, Monsieur Horbac heading

to the elevator, and me to the stairs.

"Good evening Monsieur Horbac," I offer as I start up the staircase and he enters the open elevator.

I'm almost home.

My right foot just touches the first stair as the door behind the entrance to the staircase closes with a loud slam, and I hear, "Hello again, Lucille."

*****

Following the liberation of Paris in August 1944, the fighting units of the Allied armies pushed on through Eastern France toward Germany. Some of the soldiers from these armies decided to make their way back to the City of Lights, rather than fight on the front. For most, this was a chance to get out of the fighting, keep a low profile, and simply sit out the remainder of the war. For others, this was a chance to take advantage of their military uniform to steal, assault, rape, and murder without compunction. Paris, and other liberated cities, were hit by a wave of violence and crime not often discussed after the war. Up to 50,000 American and 100,000 British soldiers deserted their units during World War II. Between June 1944 and April 1945, the US Army investigated over 7,900 cases of criminal activity. Forty-four percent of these were violence, including rape, manslaughter, and murder. Eventually, law and order were restored in the liberated cities of Europe, but it took to the end of the war, and the reintroduction of strong civilian police authorities, to make this happen.

Regime Change

Where are the Fascists?

As I zip past the finish line, I look to one side and then the other.

Where are the Fascists? There is always some Fascist official at the finish line.

I turn around to see the other racers. They have started coming in behind me.

Yes! At least two minutes ahead of the next fastest guy. Thank god Coppi is not an amateur any longer.

Francesci rides up to where I'm dismounting my bike. He looks disoriented as well. His Fascist insignia rests next to his number on his racing jersey, just as mine sits next to my number like a cancerous mole on an otherwise unblemished face.

The crowd cheers for us as we head up to the winners' circle, where a podium is set up.

"Where are the Fascists to greet us?" Francesci asks.

Without the Fascists, how do we know the race is official?

"I was thinking the same thing. They are always here!" I reply.

I better not lose this win because no Fascist bothered to show up.

Third place, Mestini, comes in; a bewildered look on his face reveals the same confusion Francesci and I expressed.

"Where have all the Fascists gone?" he asks as he climbs to join us on the podium.

The crowd is cheering, "Urra, Urra, Urra, we're free! Urra!"

Distracted, I don't answer Mestini's question.

I won. I won. Damn it, I won. I will be rewarded whether or not some Fascist scum deems it worthy to show his face!

Francesci replies, "I don't recall seeing any Fascists since around 22."

That seems about right, since I was already a kilometer ahead around that time.

As more racers approach the finish line, the town's people gather around them, tugging at their jerseys, pulling off the Fascists insignias.

"Take off the Fasci!" a distinguished civilian in a smart suit with well-groomed hair near the podium says to me before turning to say the same to Francesci and Mestini.

Why? Isn't it required to wear this for a national competition?

Francesci calls back, "What? What is going on?"

Men, women, children are all in the square, mad with joy. Smiles on their faces and cheers from their mouths overwhelm my fatigued mind.

"Take off the Fasci! Take off the Fasci! Mussolini is gone!" they yell toward the increasing collection of tired racers finishing the course.

"He's gone? Where did he go?" I demand of the fellow near the podium.

The fellow approaches me, pulling at the Fascist insignia. "He and the rest of the Fascists have been kicked out. We have a new government after all these years! You no longer have to wear these ridiculous things to race."

Everyone cheers, "Urra, Urra, Urra!"

Mussolini is gone. Who will lead us now?

The man keeps tugging at my shirt. "Take this off, you want to take this off now!"

Of course! No more Fascists. No more Fascist insignias!

I start removing my shirt just as Mestini asks, "Who will officiate the race?"

Yes, Who? I want my win!

"We saw who won, don't worry," the man replies above the cheering crowd.

"Urra, we're free of Mussolini!"

He's been Il Duce my whole life. What will happen now? We're free! What does that mean?

"Urra!" I scream out in unison with the crowd.

I always feel great after a race, but this is far better. Maybe the war is over. Maybe we can have food again. Maybe our army can come home.

"Urra, Urra, Urra!" the growing mass of humanity yells in unison.

All the fascist insignias are thrown to the ground. A pale spot now appears on every jersey where the insignias left a scar. Fascist flags are pulled down as well, all thrown into the street.

It's a new day for Italy! A new day for us all!

Francesci shouts out above the noise of the crowd, "Can we write down the rankings of the race, just to make sure we capture the order?"

"Of course, of course! It's a new day, but cycling does go on!" the man calls back.

*****

Ubaldo Pugnaloni (left)

News about the overthrow of Mussolini did not reach all Italians at the same time. Some were participating in the national cycling championship for amateurs, which wound its way through the Italian countryside on July 25, 1943, when the news began spreading throughout the country. After a full day of riding, the cyclists began arriving at the finish line, only to find no officials there to greet them. At all previous races, Fascist officials, who controlled all sports in Italy, would meet the winning cyclists, announce the prize-takers for the event, and give some speech about how sport makes society warlike (which in their view was a good thing). On this day, Ubaldo Pugnaloni, won the race while wearing the requisite Fascist insignia on his jersey. When Pugnaloni went to the winner's podium to receive his prize, he was surprised to find not a single Fascist official left to present him his award. After realizing what had transpired during the race, he quickly ripped off the Fascist insignia and joined the festivities.

Unintentional

I love these press conferences. A gaggle of re-porters crowded around me hoping to ask questions.

I am somebody.

Hands raising, my heart pounding, and sincere interest in what I have to say.

This is why I ran for office. People want to listen to me, now.

"Mr. Chairman, Mr. Chairman. How was your trip Mr. Chairman? Reporters yell above each other, hoping to get my attention.

How can they not know by now I only pick guys who ask questions I like?

"Fine, my trip was fine. Our boys in the Navy are doing a splendid job. They've learned how to slap the Japs. I can tell you, our boys have never been in bet-ter spirits."

These guys sop this stuff up.

"Mr. Chairman, Mr. Chairman, Mr. Chairman . . . Is there anything to the rumors our torpedoes are malfunctioning?"

Laughing jovially, I pause for a moment.

Damn, I was about to call on Stan! He's got the softball I am prepared to answer.

Our torpedoes. . . no problem.

"Oh, no, nothing to it. That's just rumor started by some misinformed or ill-willed person wanting to shame our brave fighting boys. Our torpedoes are working just fine. Just last month our boys in the Silent Service sank more than 20 ships, for 83,000 tons."

Not great numbers, but it's what we have with these lousy torpedoes.

"Mr. Chairman, Mr. Chairman, I have a question."

"Yes, Stan, good to see you."

"You too, sir. What did you learn of reports U.S. submarines are at risk from the Japanese because they are good sub hunters?"

"Nothing to that! Our boys are perfectly safe, because they know what they're doing."

Thanks for the softy you lousy rat.

"A Follow-up, Mr. Chairman, are you at all concerned about Japanese Depth Charges?"

Damn it Stan, I told you no follow-ups.

Jap depth charges. . . yeah, Navy told me Japs don't set them right."

"Not at all, Stan, the Japs don't set their depth charges deep enough to hit our boats. I'm not worried at all about the safety of our fine sub crews."

Another reporter chimes in, "How about logistics, are our boys in the Pacific getting everything they need to win this war?"

Oh, what a softball! I like this guy.

"Yes, oh yes! We are sending so much war material out there, it's getting so our boys must keep shooting just to not get buried by it. They've even got ice cream at every major base and on the ships. Imagine, ICE CREAM whenever ya want it. Now that's how to fight a war, ain't it boys!"

Everyone laughs.

"Yes Sir!"

"Yes indeed!"

I love this job!

Congressman Andrew Jackson May

In June 1943, after just returning from a trip to Hawaii for briefings on the war against Japan, Congressman Andrew Jackson May, Chairman of the House Military Affairs Committee, revealed to reporters Japanese anti-submarine practices were ineffective, because they set their depth charges too shallow to hit U.S. submarines. This little bit of highly actionable intelligence was then published in newspapers across the country, newspapers the Japanese read. Upon learning of their error, the Japanese immediately reset their depth charges to deeper depths.

At the end of the war, Vice Admiral Charles A. Lockwood, commander of the U.S. submarine fleet in the Pacific, linked Congressman May's statement to the loss of 10 submarines, with 80 men on each boat, for a total of 800 lost lives. The Congressman kept his seat in the following election, although karma caught up with him later. He lost the 1946 election due to a bribery scandal surrounding his campaign. In 1947, May was convicted on charges of accepting bribes for his influence in the award of munitions contracts during the war. May served nine months in prison before receiving a full pardon from President Truman in 1952.

The 800 men killed as a direct result of his comments could never be pardoned. They are still out on patrol somewhere in the vast Pacific Ocean.

Treat

We step down into the dark room, letting our eyes adjust from the bright early afternoon sun shining through the clouds outside.

Just a small bar with a simple tap and a few stools, this pub is perfect.

"A pint for me and my pal here," Florian calls out to the keep.

Oh, he may not know.

I pull out my wallet just as he's pulling out his.

"I'll pay for mine," I shudder in an undertone of insecurity requiring immediate quiet action.

"Put that away, your money is no good here," Florian announces back, without any sense of propriety.

How could he not know? It's been in all the papers.

Heads start turning our way.

"You've been away too long. Let's pay our own," I reply, hoping to make this about holding my own.

He won't have any of it. "Please, I can't let you

pay for yourself when I'm flush with cash. I can't spend at the front," he blurts out, too loud.

Oh, Florian, you sweet innocent soldier, you're getting yourself in trouble. The Law is the Law.

Luckily, the barkeep, who is now standing with two pints of beer directly before us, simply states, "Sorry lad, but the Queen won't let you treat now. National Security. Each of you will have to pay your own way for these."

Thank you, that saved me!

Florian looks at him, and then looks at me.

"What are you talking about?"

The barkeep, in simple words, answers back, "New law, meant to keep folks from blurting out se-crets. Loose lips sinking ships and all that. Right then lad."

Florian simply stands still for a moment.

Here's my chance.

I take a bill out of my wallet and place it on the counter.

The barkeep then turns to me to ask, "Want change?"

Of course, I want change!

"Yes, please," I say as Florian pulls a bill out of his wallet as well.

"Want change?" the barkeep asks Florian.

"No, thank you!" he says, while looking at me.

Ok, so you bettered me again. Fine.

"Drink your beer, you bastard," I laugh out as I bring the pint to my lips.

*****

On August 8, 1914, the British Parliament passed the Defense of the Realm Act (DORA). This law greatly increased the powers of the government for the duration of the war, giving broad powers of requisition of property, censorship, and social control mechanisms aimed at winning the war. Among the law's provisions were a ban on flying kites, starting bonfires, buying binoculars, feeding bread to wild animals, discussing any kind of military matters, buying alcohol on public transport, and most controversial, making it illegal for anyone to treat anyone else to alcohol at a pub. These measures were put in place in the belief that if people were not allowed to get others drunk, then no one would spill the national security secrets they possessed. People who broke the law with intent could be put to death. Britain was not alone in this law, as Canada passed the War Measures Act and the Emergencies Act as well. The United States passed the Sedition Act and the Espionage Act, although these did not ban anyone from treating anyone else to a beer at a pub. Most of these laws were lightened up after the end of the war.

When World War II broke out, these kinds of laws came back - In Britain, the Emergency Powers Act and the Treachery Act. However, neither of these banned treating someone else to a beer.

Unexploded

"You're Mr. B, and I'm a dragon slayer!" seven-year-old Masaki yells, as he chases me across the school playground.

These kids and their imaginations, pretending they are fighter pilots taking down American bombers while running mad across a dusty field of drying brown grass.

"I'm 20 seconds from Osaka, locking on target," I call out, so all the little dragon killers can home in on me.

"Bamm, Bamm, Bamm, Bamm, Bamm," Kosaku bursts in syncopated rhythms to match those of a 20-millimeter cannon attempting to rip through the silver skin of an American B-29.

Flapping my arm to portray a damaged wing, I belt out, "You got me, you got me, my wing is on fire."

The kids run at me, tackling me to the ground with squeals, giggles, and a few mouthed machine gun bursts for good measure.

They are in good spirits, even though we are far from home.

We roll a bit, giggling as we head toward the edge of the field. Masaki rises first, running parallel with the field's edge, brushing his arms against the wild weeds growing just beyond.

I miss my family. They must all miss theirs so much. To be so far from their mothers. Their fathers either old or away at war. At least they are usually safer here in the countryside. The bombers only come out here by accident.

The other children chase Masaki, arms stretched out to rub along the summer flush weeds.

"A bomb, a bomb, Teacher, a bomb!" Kosaku yells out, frozen in place directly before a tangled mass of weeds.

The other children gather around Kosaku, staring into the growth, hoping to catch a glimpse of a bomb.

"Stand back, children," I say gently so as not to scare them, as I approach Kosaku to see what he's talking about.

The children step back.

134

I step into Kosaku's place as he points inside the tangled weeds. "Look, right there, Teacher!"

We've been warned about what we're supposed to do when we find an unexploded bomb. Don't play with it. Don't pick it up. Call the Air Raid Warden. They will dispose of it.

"Children, what do we do when we find a bomb?" I ask of the group as I strain to see the hexagonal metallic object in the weeds. It is about half a meter long with two tons of metallic hue - one shiny, the other darker. A bit of rust seems to be forming on the end most exposed to the air.

This must have been here for some time. We should leave here if it is a bomb, marking the spot with a stick or something so we can show the Air Raid Warden.

"Kosaku, since you found the bomb, you find a stick to mark the spot. We'll then go get the Air Raid Warden."

The children cheer and start running back toward the village, yelling at the top of their lungs "A bomb, a bomb, Air Raid Warden, we found a bomb!"

This is the most excitement they've had since we were evacuated from Osaka.

As we approach the edge of the village, an old man steps out of one of the small houses. He is wearing a vest with characters signifying he is the Air Raid Warden for the area.

"What is this racket?" he demands from me, completely ignoring the children.

"Air Raid Warden, we found a bomb at the edge of the field where we were practicing air raid drills," I offer, hoping to pay due respect.

We were practicing air raid drills in a way, as I was teaching the children how to be fighter pilots.

With a huff, the Air Raid Warden stomps forward while releasing a few words, "Show me what you think is a bomb."

"Yes, Air Raid Warden, this way," I suggest, offering him my arm as a guide.

The children respectfully lead the way back toward the field.

As we approach the edge of the field in silence, I look toward Kosaku.

Perhaps he would like to show where the bomb is, since he found it.

Kosaku looks back at me, bowing a bit while lowering his eyes to show respect.

I guess not.

The Air Raid Warden sees the stick in the ground, turns to me with a look of disgust before saying, "This is it?"

"Air Raid Warden, it is in the weeds behind the stick. We placed the stick to remind us where it is."

"Of course you did," he replies.

"Go in and get it," he orders.

I look at him, confused.

Does he want me to go into the weeds to fetch out the bomb?

He looks back at me, shoving his shoulders and arms forward to signify forward movement.

Yes, he wants me to go in to get it.

"Air Raid Warden, how should I handle it?" I ask, hoping not to have to admit that I don't know what I'm doing.

"You are a teacher?" he says in a most disrespect-ful way before diving into the bush himself.

Yes, I am a teacher and I want to make sure these kids are safe.

"Children, let's step back to give the Air Raid Warden some space to work," I suggest to the very quiet and eager children formed up in a neat half circle two paces off.

Out of the corner of my eye, I see the metallic object flying toward the children.

Why is it in the air? Did the Air Raid Warden throw it?

As it sails through the air I hear the words, "It's a dud, see!" coming from within the weeds.

The incendiary bomb lands right in front of the children before exploding into a fiery ball of flame.

My whole world is engulfed in red, orange, then black hues, before I lose sight completely. Screams from young voices envelop all other sounds.

The children, how hurt are they?

I hear nothing more as I fade into emptiness.

*****

An American Incendiary Device

B-29s were called B-San (Mr. B) by the Japanese out of grudging respect for the American bombers.

B-29s dropping Incendiary Bombs on Japan

In July 1945, a group of children and their teacher, who had been evacuated out of Osaka for their safety, were playing on the playground of their new school located in a small village over 40 miles from their homes and families. When the group found an unexploded incendiary cluster from an American bomb, they notified the local Air Raid Warden. The warden, who did not believe the device to be live, threw it to show the kids. Unfortunately, he was wrong. The bomb went off, killing eight of the children outright and fatally wounding the teacher and another child.

Often those trying to escape war have it come back to find them. This is true even long after the guns fall silent. To this day, unexploded bombs and other munitions litter the battlefields and civilian countryside, across vast swaths of the world. Old bombs kill hundreds of people every year. War never stops finding ways to kill.

Candy Bomber

Few notice them anymore,

The urchins of the street staring up at the metal streaming through the air,

Each grimy youth covered in torn clothes atop a starving frame of muscle and bone.

Too young to have much of a memory of the war,

Old enough to build a memory of now,

Their faces lifted to the sky,

They hope,

They dream,

They plead,

This one. . .,

This one. . .,

This one. . ., until out of a cockpit window of one in the line of C-47's, small objects fall to the earth.

A mad scramble,

A dash through the rubble-strewn streets,

Shimmering sun glistening off the morning dew through which they fall is blocked by the broken masonry of a bombed-out wall.

Arms flail,

Legs kick out,

The small scurry,

The bigger force,

The oldest and heaviest crush.

Not enough for everyone, even though some have stores in their pockets.

Out of the scrum, the urchins break free,

Pulling open wrappers,

Breaking off pieces,

Sharing with those who did not prevail.

Smiles replace frowns for a moment,

Kindness steps in for greed,

Faces turn skyward again,

New Hope,

New Life,

From those who just a few years before were dropping a far more menacing item upon the city.

A thanks to a former foe, who now offers chocolate while delivering coal for heat.

A new war, Cold as it may be,

Warming the heart to know friends are out there,

Just over 100 miles away,

Sending what they can,

So we may live,

And throwing in a little something sweet,

We may love.

*****

Children watching a transport plane over Berlin

On June 24, 1948, the Soviet occupation authorities in Eastern Germany, within which Berlin was a
divided city occupied by the four victors of World
War II, announced a complete shutdown of all rail
and road traffic to the non-Soviet occupied zones.
What became known as the Berlin Blockade was an
attempt by the Soviets to force the other occupying
powers out of Berlin. In defiance of this blockade,
the United States, United Kingdom, and France began a massive airlift to feed, clothe, and heat the cut-
off city.

Flying into the remaining two airports, and even
landing flying boats along a Berlin river, a steady

stream of transport aircraft delivered food, coal, and clothing while whisking out the sick, malnourished, and persecuted from across Europe who had ended up in the Western Zone of Berlin. For almost a year, the Berlin Airlift provided hope and life to a city separated from the rest of the world. This was the first major crisis and test of the West in the Cold War.

By May 12, 1949, the Soviets realized the Blockade had failed. In that time, more than 1.5 million tons of coal, food, clothing and other life-essential goods had been flown into West Berlin, while more than 50,000 people were airlifted out. The citizens of that part of the city were now eating more calories per day than they had before the blockade began.

Watching a transport land in Berlin

Rather than force the western powers out of Berlin, the blockade solidified their desire to stay, providing a motivating force to come together, unify their zones of occupation, and give the people of the city hope in themselves, their role in a new West Germany, and a future they could build together. On May 12, 1949, the Soviets reopened the road and rail routes to Berlin, ending the blockade.

Shoot Down

"You seeing this?" Captain Moore yells as he points left out the cockpit window.

Stepping forward, away from the center of the Huey, I lean out the open left side door, where a sight straight out of a history book greets me.

Four huge green bi-planes, flying in formation, are cruising just over Site 85, dropping explosives on and around the radar base there.

How'd they know it was here?

"I'm gonna get above them. You grab a gun. Let's see if we can have a little fun!" Moore yells into the comms again.

Scrambling back from the open side door, I reach down with my right hand to unstrap one of the AK-47s we brought with us on this re-supply mission.

The front strap lock on the AKs sticks a bit, forcing me to kneel to get better leverage to pull up on it.

Damn, I don't want to miss my chance to shoot at a bi-plane!

While kneeling, I notice the treetops fade away

from just below the open right-side door of the Huey.

We're getting up there.

Catching the strap lock, I'm able to snap it open, freeing the AKs from their safe storage.

I yank out the AK on top.

Do I strap them back in, or turn and shoot, leaving the AKs loose?

I turn my head to look out the left side door. The bi-planes are still there, in formation, as they head away from the radar base.

They must not have seen us yet.

I'm not missing them yet.

Holding the free AK under my arm, I re-strap the remaining guns to make sure they don't start falling about the Huey's rocking cabin.

Alright, they're good to go. Now for some fun!

Swinging back around so I'm facing out the open left side of the Huey, I point the AK-47 toward the last plane in the formation.

No aiming with this thing!

The AK set to semi-automatic, I pump quite a

few rounds toward the slow bi-plane trudging just be-low.

Did I even hit anything?

Banking left, the plane breaks formation.

I must have got his attention.

Moore yells from the cockpit, "Let's make this a dogfight!" as he banks us to follow the bi-plane.

Yeah, let's get this gook!

Securing myself against the Huey's bulkhead, I fire off more rounds at the fleeing bi-plane.

Nowhere to go buddy! Nowhere to hide!

Unloading round after round into the bi-plane, my cartridge empties out quick.

Whether or not I'm hitting anything, he's running scared.

This is fun!

A second bi-plane comes into view as I pull out the empty cartridge, replacing it with a full one from my vest pocket.

He must be following the plane I'm shooting at.

This one has a gun-mount on top, with a guy inside firing something up toward us.

Hey, they're shooting back. Now it's a fight!

"Focus on the shooter!" Moore yells.

"Already on it!" I yell back.

He probably didn't hear me.

No matter.

I lock the new cartridge into the AK, pull back to load the first round in the chamber, and let loose on the second bi-plane.

He's staying level so his guy can shoot. Thanks man!

ZZZZzzzttt, ZZZZzzzttt, ZZZZzzzttt. Rounds whiz by me.

Maybe I shouldn't be that thankful yet?

Just as that thought crosses my mind, smoke begins seeping, then spewing forth from the armed bi-plane.

I must have hit something!

Slowly at first, then faster and faster, the large green machine from the past descends toward the earth.

"Woods, you got 'em!" Moore yells on the comms.

I shot down a bi-plane!

"Let's get the other one!" I yell, hoping Moore can hear me.

Looking around for the first bi-plane, I can see him from the right side scrambling, at what low speed he can, to get back to Vietnamese airspace.

Moore banks the Huey to the right.

I'll get you yet, my pretty!

Lunging across the open deck of the Huey, I jump the tether connecting me to the helicopter as I swing the AK-47 up to fire from the open right door.

"There he is!" Moore yells, just as I see the scurrying bi-plane.

Pumping rounds into this guy, I'm surprised when it starts nose-diving toward the ground.

No smoke.

The plane simply descends, no turning, no attempt to pull up, nothing.

"Seems like we're done here." Moore yells, "Gotta land this ammo."

What about the other two?

"Hey, I'm 2/5th of the way to Ace!" I yell back.

"Good shootin' Woods!" Moore exclaims as he banks the Huey back toward the radar station. "The other two bugged out. Can't catch 'em with all this ammo aboard."

Two ain't bad, even if they were bi-planes!

*****

A Huey in Vietnam

On January 12, 1968, an American helicopter, part of the Air America CIA sponsored mission, was running supplies of ammunition to a secret U.S. Air Force radar station high-up in the hills of northern Laos. Coming through the canyon near the base, the Americans were surprised to find four Vietnamese An-2 bi-planes in the process of bombing the radar station. The American helicopter flew in above the Vietnamese planes, a crew member shooting at them with a hand-held AK-47. Two of the bi-planes went down in the jungles, while the other two were able to get away. Two months later the radar station was attacked by Vietnamese ground units, with a complete loss of all U.S. personnel serving at the station. This represented the greatest loss of life in a single engagement for the U.S. Air Force during the Vietnam War.

https://www.cia.gov/library/center-for-the-study-of-intelligence/csi-publications/csi-studies/studies/vol52no2/iac/an-air-combat-first.html

Afterword

All the stories in this collection are based on real events. Since the individuals involved could not be interviewed, everything written here is fiction. The human story, as we know it, is fiction wrapped around actual events. Little can be known for sure, even by those present in the moment of the event. Attempting to come to the truth simply involves choosing a narrative to believe.

When we weave all our stories together, we come up with something far more profound than anything we could have created alone. We come up with the rich tapestry of human history.

This is the fourth of what will hopefully be many collections from The 20th Century's War. Building from World War I and World War II, this collection has one story from the Vietnam War. Yet, there is so much more to write about. Other episodes will cover stories from Korea, as well as Vietnam, the wars in the Balkans, the Russian Revolution, multiple conflicts in Afghanistan, and all the flare-ups in the Middle East since 1898.

Unfortunately, The 20th Century's War is not yet over. Our modern human story of wanton waste is still being written.

I sincerely hope you enjoyed reading this book as much as I enjoyed writing it. If you did, I would greatly appreciate a short review on your favorite book website. Reviews are crucial for any author, and even just a line or two can make a huge difference. Thank you. -Jeremy

Get Threads of The War, Volume I-IV Free

http://eepurl.com/cq0l_H

Other books by Jeremy Strozer

Threads of The War, Volume I

Threads of The War, Volume II

Threads of The War, Volume III

About the Author

Jeremy R. Strozer

Raised in California, Jeremy moved to the Washington, D.C. area at the age of 18 to attend university. Through education and luck, he became a Fulbright Fellow, a Presidential Management Fellow, and found ways to live and work across vast swaths of the world. Professionally, Jeremy helped remove unexploded ordnance from war-ravaged

countries; stem the flow of the world's most danger-
ous weapons; and potentially reduced the likelihood
of war between a couple of the world's most powerful countries.

He lives in Falls Church, Virginia, with his wife,
son and daughter, where he continues to work on pre-
venting future war and warning the world about the
human cost of violence.

**If you like what you've just read, please con-
sider following Jeremy at:**

JeremyStrozer.com

https://www.facebook.com/jeremystrozerauthor/

Twitter: @jeremystrozer

**Sponsoring Jeremy's writing and podcast
on Patreon**

https://www.patreon.com/jeremystrozer

Joining The 20th Century's War Group

http://jeremystrozer.com/group

www.ingramcontent.com/pod-product-compliance
Lightning Source LLC
Chambersburg PA
CBHW021020120726
47905CB00009B/3106